Inky the Indigo Fairy

Special thanks to
Marinder Dhani

No part of this publication may be reproduced
in whole or in part, or stored in a retrieval
system, or transmitted in any form or by any
means, electronic, mechanical, photocopying,
recording, or otherwise, without written permission
of the publisher. For information regarding
permission, write to Working Partners Limited,
1 Albion Place, London W6 OQT, United Kingdom.

Inky
the Indigo
Fairy

by Daisy Meadows
illustrated by Georgie Ripper

SCHOLASTIC INC.

New York   Toronto   London   Auckland   Sydney
Mexico City   New Delhi   Hong Kong   Buenos Aires

Cold winds blow and thick ice forms,
I conjure up this fairy storm.
To seven corners of the mortal world
the Rainbow Fairies will be hurled!

I curse every part of Fairyland,
with a frosty wave of my icy hand.
For now and always, from this fateful day,
Fairyland will be cold and gray!

Ruby, Amber, Sunny, Fern, and Sky
have been found. Now Rachel
and Kirsty must find
Inky the Indigo Fairy

Contents

A Fairytale Beginning

"Rain, rain, go away." Rachel Walker sighed. "Come again another day!"

She and her friend Kirsty Tate stared out of the attic window. Raindrops splashed against the glass, and the sky was full of purplish-black clouds.

"Isn't it a horrible day?" Kirsty said. "But it's nice and cozy in here."

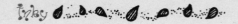

She looked around Rachel's small attic bedroom. There was just enough room for a brass bed and a patchwork quilt, a comfy armchair, and an old bookshelf.

"You know what the weather on Rainspell is like," Rachel pointed out. "It might be hot and sunny very soon!"

Both girls had come to Rainspell Island on vacation. The Walkers were staying in Mermaid Cottage, while the Tates were in Dolphin Cottage next door.

Kirsty frowned. "Yes, but what about Inky the Indigo Fairy?" she asked. "We have to find her today."

Rachel and Kirsty shared a wonderful secret. They were trying to find the seven Rainbow Fairies, who had been cast out of Fairyland by evil Jack Frost. Fairyland would be cold and gray until all seven fairies had been found again.

Rachel thought of Ruby, Amber, Sunny, Fern, and Sky, who were all safe now in the pot-at-the-end-of-the-rainbow. They had only Inky the Indigo Fairy and Heather the Violet Fairy left to find. But how could they look for them while they were stuck indoors?

"Remember what the Fairy Queen said?" she reminded Kirsty.

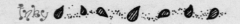

Kirsty nodded. "She said the magic would come to us." Suddenly, she looked scared. "Maybe the rain is Jack Frost's magic. Maybe he's trying to stop us from finding Inky."

"Oh no!" Rachel said. "Let's hope it stops soon. But what should we do while we're waiting?"

Kirsty thought for a moment. Then, she went over to the bookshelf. It was filled with dusty old books, and she pulled one

out. It was so big that she had to use two hands to hold it. "*The Big Book of Fairy Tales*," Rachel read out loud, looking at the cover.

"If we can't find fairies, at least we can read about them!" Kirsty grinned.

The two girls sat down on the bed and put the book on their knees. Kirsty was about to turn to the first page when Rachel gasped. "Kirsty, look at the cover! It's purple. A really deep purplish-blue."

"That's indigo," Kirsty whispered. "Oh, Rachel! Do you think Inky could be trapped inside?"

"Let's see," Rachel said. "Hurry up, Kirsty. Open the book!"

But Kirsty had spotted something else. "Rachel," she said shakily. "It's *glowing*."

Rachel looked. Kirsty was right. Some pages in the middle of the book were gleaming with a soft bluey-purple light.

Kirsty opened the book. The ink on the pages was glowing indigo. For a moment Kirsty thought that Inky might fly out of the pages, but there was no sign of her. On the first page was a picture of a wooden soldier. Above the picture were the words: *The Nutcracker.*

"Oh!" Rachel said. "I know this story. I went to see the ballet at Christmas."

"What's it about?" Kirsty asked.

"Well, a girl named Clara gets a wooden nutcracker soldier for Christmas," Rachel explained. "He comes to life and takes her to the Land of Sweets." They looked down at a brightly colored picture of a Christmas tree. A little girl was asleep beside it, holding a wooden soldier.

On the next page there was a picture of snowflakes whirling and swirling through a dark forest. "Aren't the pictures great?" Kirsty said. "The snow looks so real."

Rachel frowned. For a moment, she thought the snowflakes were moving. Gently, she put out her hand and touched the page. It felt cold and wet!

"Kirsty," she whispered. "It *is* real!" She held out her hand. There were white snowflakes on her fingers.

Kirsty looked down at the book
again, her eyes wide. The
snowflakes started to swirl
from the book's pages, right
into the bedroom, slowly at
first, then faster and faster.
Soon the snowstorm was so
thick, Rachel and Kirsty
couldn't see a thing. But
they could feel themselves
being swept up into the air
by the spinning snow cloud.

Rachel yelled to Kirsty, "Why haven't
we hit the bedroom ceiling?"

Kirsty reached for Rachel's hand.
"Because it's magic!" she whispered.

The Land of Sweets

Suddenly, the snowflakes stopped swirling. Rachel and Kirsty found themselves standing in a forest, with their backpacks at their feet. Tall trees loomed around them and crisp white snow covered the ground. They certainly weren't in Rachel's bedroom anymore.

Then Rachel realized where they were.

"Kirsty, this is the forest that was in the picture," she said, grabbing her friend's arm. "We're *inside* the book!"

Kirsty looked even more scared. "Do you think Jack Frost brought us here?" she asked. "Or his goblins?" Jack Frost's goblins were always trying to stop Rachel and Kirsty from finding the Rainbow Fairies.

"I don't know," Rachel replied. Then, she frowned. There was something odd about this snow. She bent down and gently touched a snowdrift. "This isn't snow." She laughed. "It's powdered sugar!"

"What?" Kirsty looked amazed. She scooped up a handful and tasted it. The powdered sugar was cool and sweet.

"Maybe this isn't Jack Frost's magic after all," Rachel said. "I wonder where this forest is."

"What's that?" Kirsty asked, pointing.

Rachel could see a pink and gold glow through the trees. "Let's go and find out," she said.

They picked up their backpacks and set
off. It was hard walking through the
powdered sugar. Soon their sneakers were
covered in the sugary snow.

Crack!

Rachel nearly jumped out of her skin
as a loud noise echoed through the trees.

"Sorry," said Kirsty. "I stepped on a
twig."

"Wait," Rachel whispered. "I just heard
voices!"

"Goblins?" Kirsty whispered back,
looking scared again.

Rachel listened. The voices were louder now. She sighed with relief. "No, they sound too sweet and soft to be goblins' voices."

Rachel and Kirsty hurried toward the edge of the forest. When they came out of the trees, they saw that the glow was coming from a dazzling pink and gold archway.

"Look, Kirsty." Rachel gasped. "It's made of candy!"

Kirsty stared. The archway was made of pink marshmallows and golden toffees.

Then they heard the voices again. They
spun around to see who it was. Two
people dressed in fluffy, white coats were
chatting to each other and scooping
powdered sugar into shiny metal buckets.
They had round, rosy cheeks and little,
pointy ears. They were so busy they
hadn't noticed Rachel and Kirsty yet.

"I think they're elves," Kirsty whispered.
"But they're the same size as we are. That
means we must be fairy- or, at least, elf-
sized again."

"We haven't got any wings this time,
though," Rachel whispered back.

Suddenly, one of the elves spotted them. She looked very surprised. "Hello!" she called. "Where did you come from?"

"I'm Rachel and this is Kirsty," Rachel explained. "We came here through the forest."

"Where are we?" Kirsty asked.

"This is the entrance to the Land of Sweets," said the first elf. "My name is Wafer, and this is my sister, Cone."

"We're the ice-cream makers," added Cone. "What are you doing here?"

"We're looking for Inky the Indigo Fairy," Kirsty told them. "Have you seen her?"

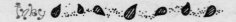

Both elves shook their heads. "We've heard of the Rainbow Fairies," said Wafer. "But Fairyland is far away from here, across the Lemonade Ocean."

"Maybe you should ask the Sugarplum Fairy for help," Cone suggested. "She's so smart and kind, she'll know what to do. She lives on the other side of the village."

"Could you take us to her?" Rachel asked eagerly.

The elves nodded. "Follow us," they said together. And they led Rachel and

Kirsty through the archway of pink and gold sweets.

On the other side of the arch, the sun shone down warmly from a bright blue sky. Flowers made of strawberry cream grew beneath milk-chocolate trees. Squishy pink and white marshmallow houses lined the village street, which was paved with jelly beans.

"Isn't this great?" Kirsty laughed. "It's like being inside a giant candy store!"

"And it all looks *yummy!*" Rachel agreed, spotting a garden gate made of peppermint sticks.

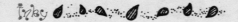

There were elves
hurrying everywhere.
Some had shiny
buckets like the ice-
cream makers, and others carried tiny,
silver hammers. There were gingerbread
men, too, looking very stylish in their
bright bow ties and currant buttons. Then
a whole line of tiny wooden soldiers in
polished black boots marched across the
street in front of them, and Rachel
spotted a glistening pink sugar mouse
scurrying between their feet. Kirsty and
Rachel smiled at each other with delight.

The two elves led Rachel and Kirsty

down the street. Suddenly, an angry-
looking gingerbread man hurried out of
one of the houses and bumped into Cone.

"Hello, Buttons," Wafer said. "You're in
a hurry."

"What's the matter?" Cone asked. "You
look upset."

The gingerbread man held out
his hand. "Look at my best
bow tie!" he said. "It was red
when I hung it out to dry
on my clothesline, and
now it's *this* color!"

Rachel and Kirsty gasped. The bow tie
was purplish-blue!

"Inky!" they both said together.

The ice-cream elves looked puzzled.

"I think this means that Inky the
Indigo Fairy is close by," Rachel
explained.

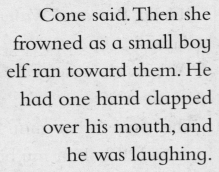

"We'd better help you find her before
she gets into any more trouble,"
Cone said. Then she
frowned as a small boy
elf ran toward them. He
had one hand clapped
over his mouth, and
he was laughing.

"Scoop!" called Wafer. She turned to
Rachel and Kirsty. "He's our little brother,"
she explained. "Scoop, what are you
giggling about?"

Still laughing, Scoop took his hand away from his mouth. Rachel and Kirsty stared. The little elf's mouth was stained indigo!

"What happened?" Cone gasped.

"I had a drink from the lemonade fountain," Scoop said between giggles. "All the lemonade's turned purplish-blue. It made my tongue tingle, too!"

"That sounds like more Rainbow Fairy magic!" Kirsty said.

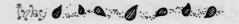

"Where's the lemonade fountain?"
Rachel asked the elves.

"In the village square," replied Cone.
"Just around the corner."

"Thanks for your help," said Kirsty.
She grabbed Rachel's hand and they ran
off.

As soon as Rachel and Kirsty
rounded the corner, they skidded to a
halt. In the middle of the village square
was a pretty fountain. Bright purplish-
blue liquid bubbled up from a fountain
shaped like a dolphin. A crowd of elves,
soldiers, and gingerbread men stood
around the fountain, all talking at once.
They sounded angry. A polka-dotted
jack-in-the-box bounced back and forth
with a grumpy look on his face.

A swirl of indigo fairy dust shot up
from the middle of the crowd. As the
dust fell to the ground, it changed into
blackberry-scented inkdrops.

Rachel and Kirsty stared at each
other in delight. They knew what fairy
dust meant. They had found another
Rainbow Fairy!

Look Out!

"Inky!" Rachel called as she and Kirsty pushed their way through the crowd. "Is that you?"

"Who's that?" called a sassy, tinkling voice.

Inky was standing by the edge of the lemonade fountain. She had neat blue-black hair and twinkling, dark blue eyes. She was dressed in indigo denim jeans and a matching jacket, covered with sparkly patches. Inkdrop-shaped silver earrings hung from her ears, and her wand was indigo, tipped with silver.

The fairy stared at Rachel and Kirsty with her hands on her hips. "Who are you?" she asked. "And how do you know my name?"

"I'm Kirsty, and this is Rachel," Kirsty explained. "We've come to take you back to your Rainbow sisters."

"We've found five of your sisters so far,"
Rachel added. "We're going to help you
all go home to Fairyland."

"That's wonderful
news!" Inky cried.
"I've been so
worried."

"How did you get
to the Land of
Sweets?" Kirsty asked.

"The wind blew me
down the chimney of
Mermaid Cottage,
and into the story of
The Nutcracker," Inky replied. "I've been in
the Land of Sweets ever since. I can't go
back to Fairyland and break Jack Frost's
spell without my sisters. I have to get
back to Rainspell Island first."

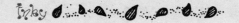

Before Rachel and Kirsty could say anything else, the crowd started shouting again.

"Look what she's done to the lemonade fountain!" grumbled one elf.

Inky grinned at him. "I didn't mean to," she said. "The lemonade looked so yummy, I just had to have a drink. And that's when it turned indigo."

"And what about my bow tie?" snapped Buttons. He had followed Kirsty and Rachel to the fountain.

"I was really tired after walking out of the forest," Inky explained.

"I borrowed your lovely bow tie to wrap around me while I had a little nap."

The crowd started to mutter angrily again.

Quickly, Rachel stepped forward. "Wait," she said. "Have you heard about the Rainbow Fairies and Jack Frost's spell?"

The crowd listened as Rachel told them the whole story. When she'd finished, they didn't look angry anymore.

"I'm *so* sorry for all the trouble I've caused," Inky said. "Please, can you tell us how to get back to Rainspell Island?"

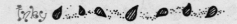

"The Sugarplum Fairy will help you," said the jack-in-the-box, with a little bounce. "Her home is just past the jelly bean fields."

"That's where we were going," Kirsty said.

"Come on, then!" Inky cried. She darted forward and took Rachel and Kirsty by the hand.

"Good luck!" called everyone.

Rachel and Kirsty walked along the
road toward the jelly bean fields with
Inky darting eagerly ahead of them. Just
outside the village was a huge rock of
golden toffee, as tall as a marshmallow
house. Elves were tapping the rock with
little hammers to break pieces off the
toffee. Other elves picked them up and
put them into silver buckets.

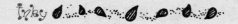

Kirsty nudged Rachel. "That looks like hard work," she said. "They don't seem to be collecting much toffee at all!"

Rachel peeped into one of the buckets as an elf walked past. Kirsty was right. There were only a few chips of toffee in it.

"Is there something wrong with the toffee?" Inky wondered.

The elf with the bucket overheard her.

"It's really hard today," he grumbled. "Anyone would think it had been *frozen*."

"Frozen!" Kirsty said in alarm. "Do you think that means Jack Frost's goblins are here, in the Land of Sweets?"

Whenever the goblins were close by, they brought frost and icy weather.

Inky looked scared. "I hope not," she said.

Just then, a loud, rumbling noise and a shout of "Look out!" made them all jump. An enormous wooden barrel was rolling down the street, straight toward them! And running behind it were two goblins, grinning all over their ugly faces.

Stop Those Goblins!

"We've got you now, Inky!" shouted one of the goblins.

For a moment everyone froze. Then Inky leaped into action and gave Rachel and Kirsty a push. "Quick! Get out of the way!" she yelled.

They jumped aside just in time. The elves dropped their hammers and buckets.

They dashed out of the way, bumping
into one another in their panic.

Crash!

The barrel smashed right into the toffee
mountain. Then it burst open. Lemon
sherbet spilled out in a sticky yellow cloud.

"Inky! Kirsty!" Rachel coughed, peering
through the sherbet. "Are you all right?"

"I think so!" Kirsty sneezed. *"Aachoo!"*

"HELP!"

Kirsty heard Inky's frightened voice. But she couldn't see her through the sherbet cloud.

"Help!" Inky shouted again. "The goblins have got me!" Her voice was getting fainter.

"Quick, Rachel!" Kirsty gasped. "Have you got our magic bags?"

Still coughing, Rachel swung her backpack around. Titania, the Fairy Queen, had given the girls bags full of magic gifts to help them rescue the missing Rainbow Fairies.

Rachel opened her backpack. Inside it, one of the magic bags was glowing, faintly silver. Rachel pulled out a folded paper fan from the bag. Puzzled, she opened the fan up. It was colored like the most beautiful rainbow, with stripes of red, orange, yellow, green, blue, indigo, and violet.

Rachel thought for a moment. Then she began to flap the fan at the clouds of sherbet.

Whoosh!

A blast of air from the fan blew almost all of the sherbet away.

"Wow! This fan is amazing!" Rachel gasped as the last of the sherbet drifted off.

"Look, Rachel!" shouted Kirsty.
"They're over there!"

The goblins had tied Inky's sneakers
together with strawberry shoelaces. They
were half-dragging, half-carrying her
up the road, toward the jelly bean fields.

"We've got to save her," Rachel said,
quickly folding the fan and putting it in
her pocket. "Come on, Kirsty!"

"I'll go and tell the Sugarplum
Fairy," said one of the elves, and he
dashed off.

Rachel and
Kirsty ran up the
road. The goblins
had a head start,
but Inky was
wriggling so
much that she
was slowing
them down.

The road led
through the jelly
bean fields. Tall
green plants
stood in rows,
each one covered
with different-colored beans — pink,
white, blue-spotted, and chocolate-brown
ones. Elves were picking the jelly beans
and putting them into big baskets.

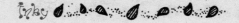

Suddenly, Rachel noticed that the goblins were looking greedily at the jelly beans. One of them skidded to a halt. He leaned over the fence and grabbed a big jelly bean from the nearest plant. The other goblin did the same.

"Yummy!" said the first goblin, stuffing the bean into his mouth.

"They're so greedy!" Rachel panted.

"Yes, but it gives us a chance to trick them!" Kirsty puffed. She started to run even faster.

The elves working in the field shouted angrily at the goblins. But that didn't stop them. They gobbled down one bean after another, picking beans with one hand and holding on to Inky with the other.

"I've got an idea," Rachel whispered to Kirsty. At the side of the road she could see some baskets full of beans that had already been picked. She hurried over and lifted up a basket. Then she held it out toward the goblins.

"Look what I've got," she called. "A whole basketful of beans!"

A Very Suitable Punishment

The goblins' eyes lit up when they saw the basket. Inky grinned and winked at Kirsty and Rachel. She'd guessed what they were doing.

"Those jelly beans look yummy," Inky said to the goblins. "I wish I could have one."

"Be quiet," snapped the goblin with the bigger nose. He turned to the other goblin. "You keep hold of the fairy while I get the beans."

"No," said the other one. "You'll eat all the beans! You hold the fairy, and *I'll* get the beans."

"No!" roared the first goblin. "Then *you'll* eat all the beans!"

Glaring at each other, both goblins let go of Inky and ran toward Rachel.

She quickly threw a handful of beans on the ground and backed away.

The goblins bent down to grab the beans. When they stood up again, Rachel threw another handful back down the hill, away from Inky.

48

Those greedy goblins just couldn't resist
the yummy beans!

While the goblins were busy stuffing
themselves, Kirsty rushed over to untie
Inky. "Are you all right?" she asked.

Inky nodded and wriggled her feet.
"Thank you!"

Rachel put the basket on the ground
and ran over to Kirsty and Inky. The
goblins pounced on the basket and began
squabbling over the rest of the beans.

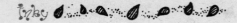

"Let's get out of here!" Rachel said.

Suddenly, there was a gentle flapping
noise overhead. Rachel looked up to see
a huge butterfly with pink and gold
wings fluttering above them. On its back
sat a fairy with long, red hair.

The butterfly landed gently on the ground. The fairy climbed off the butterfly's back and smiled at Inky and the girls. She wore a long green and gold dress and a tiara.

"Welcome," she said. "I am the Sugarplum Fairy." She looked sternly at the goblins who were crouching beside the empty bean basket. "What are *you* doing in the Land of Sweets?" she demanded.

The goblins didn't answer. They were too busy groaning and holding their tummies.

"Oooh!" moaned the one with the big nose. "My tummy hurts."

"Mine too," whined the other one. "I feel sick."

"They've eaten too many jelly beans!" Inky grinned at Rachel and Kirsty.

The Sugarplum Fairy looked even angrier. "Since you have stolen so many of our delicious jelly beans," she said to the goblins, "you must be taught a lesson."

"Why don't you make them pick jelly beans?" Inky suggested.

"What a good idea." The Sugarplum Fairy smiled.

"That doesn't seem like a very bad punishment," Kirsty whispered to Rachel.

"But just look at the goblins' faces," Rachel whispered back.

The goblins looked horrified at the thought of more jelly beans! They tried to get up, as if they wanted to run away. But the Sugarplum Fairy waved her hand and several elves came running out of the jelly bean fields. They marched the goblins into the nearest field and handed them empty baskets. With sulky faces, the goblins started to pick the beans.

"Serves them right!" laughed Inky. Then she looked worried again. "But I still need to get back to my Rainbow sisters."

"Please, can you help us get back to Rainspell Island?" Rachel asked the Sugarplum Fairy.

The beautiful fairy nodded. "We will send you home by balloon!" she said. She waved her wand at the empty bean basket. Rachel and Kirsty watched in amazement as it grew bigger and bigger.

"There is your basket."

"But where's the balloon?" said Rachel.

The Sugarplum
Fairy pointed to a
tall tree, covered with
pink blossoms.

"What pretty flowers,"
Kirsty said. Then she took
a closer look and began to laugh.
"They're not flowers. They're pieces of
bubble gum!"

"How is that going to help?" Rachel
felt puzzled.

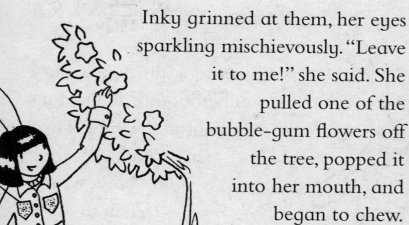

Inky grinned at them, her eyes
sparkling mischievously. "Leave
it to me!" she said. She
pulled one of the
bubble-gum flowers off
the tree, popped it
into her mouth, and
began to chew.

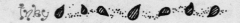
Then, screwing up her
face, she blew a huge,
pink bubble-gum
bubble. She puffed
and puffed, and
the bubble grew
bigger and
bigger. Soon, it towered
above them. It was the
biggest bubble-gum
bubble Rachel and
Kirsty had
ever seen!
Inky took the bubble out
of her mouth, and tied a
knot in the end. "The
perfect balloon!" she
said. "Now, we're
ready to go."

Rachel and Kirsty grinned at each other. What a wonderful way to travel back to Rainspell!

The elves working in the jelly bean fields, and the elves who had followed Rachel and Kirsty out of the village, helped to tie the bubble-gum balloon to the basket. Then, Rachel, Kirsty, and Inky climbed inside.

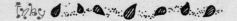

The Sugarplum Fairy waved her wand at the balloon, showering it with gold sparkles.

"The balloon will take you to Rainspell Island," she explained. "Good-bye, and good luck."

"Thank you," called Rachel and Inky. But Kirsty was looking around in dismay. "There's no wind!" she said. "We won't be able to get off the ground!"

The Bubble-gum Balloon

Rachel looked at the leaves on the
bubble-gum tree. Kirsty was right. They
weren't moving at all.

The Sugarplum Fairy smiled. "Rachel,
don't you remember what you have in
your pocket?" she said.

"Of course!" Rachel exclaimed. "The
magic fan!" She took it out of her pocket

and unfolded it. Then, she flapped it
under the balloon.

Whoosh!

The blast of air lifted the balloon

up into the sky.
"Good-bye!" Kirsty
called, waving at the
Sugarplum Fairy
and all the elves.
"Thank you for all
your help," Inky
called. "Sorry I made
such a mess!" she added
with a giggle.

The balloon bobbed
slowly upward. As it got higher,
the wind became stronger, so Rachel
put away the fan. Big, puffy clouds began
swirling around the balloon.

"We'll be home soon," Rachel said,
trying to sound cheerful.

The wind roared around them, rocking
the basket from side to side. Rachel,
Kirsty, and Inky hung on to one another.

Then, all of a sudden, the wind
dropped. The balloon stopped swaying.
The air felt warm.

Kirsty opened her eyes. "We're home!"
she gasped.

They were back in Rachel's attic
bedroom at Mermaid Cottage. The
balloon and the basket had vanished. The
book of fairy tales was lying on the floor,
open at *The Nutcracker*.

"But where's Inky?" Rachel said.

"I'm in here!" said a sassy voice. The Indigo Fairy popped up from Rachel's pocket. She wriggled out and fluttered into the air, her wings sparkling with rainbows and showering the room with fairy dust inkdrops. The smell of blackberries drifted up as they popped.

Kirsty picked up the book. She turned the pages until she found a picture of the Land of Sweets. "It's a shame we didn't get to taste any of that wonderful candy," she said.

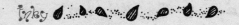

As she spoke, a tiny puff of powdered sugar floated out of the book. Then, a shower of different-colored jelly beans fell onto Rachel's bed.

"They must be a present from the Sugarplum Fairy!" Inky laughed.

Rachel and Kirsty each popped a jelly bean into their mouths. They were tiny, but they tasted delicious!

"Yum!" said Inky, munching a bean. "Can we take some back to the pot for my sisters?"

Rachel nodded. "Let's go right away," she said, filling her pockets with beans. "Your sisters will be waiting for you." She looked at Kirsty and smiled. They had rescued another fairy and escaped the goblins once again. They'd even been inside a fairy story in a book. And, now, there was only one more fairy to find!

All the Rainbow Fairies are together, except one! But they'll never get their Rainbow Magic back without

Heather the Violet Fairy

Message on a Kite

"I can't believe this is the last day of our vacation!" said Rachel Walker. She gazed up at her kite as it rose in the clear blue sky.

Kirsty Tate watched the purple kite soar above the field beside Mermaid Cottage. "But we still have to find Heather!" she reminded Rachel.

Jack Frost's wicked spell had banished the seven Rainbow Fairies to Rainspell Island. And without the Rainbow Fairies, Fairyland had no color! Kirsty and Rachel had already found Ruby, Amber, Sunny, Fern, Sky, and Inky. Now there was just Heather the Violet Fairy left to find.

Rachel felt the kite tug on its string. She looked up. Something violet and silver flashed at the end of the kite's long tail. "Look up there!" she shouted.

Kirsty shaded her eyes with her hand. "What is it? Do you think it's a fairy?" she asked.

"I'm not sure," Rachel said, winding in the string.

As the kite came bobbing toward them, Kirsty saw that a long piece of

violet-colored ribbon was tied to its tail.
She helped Rachel untie the ribbon and
smooth it out.

"It has tiny silver writing on it," Rachel
said.

Read the rest of

RAINBOW magic

Heather the **Violet Fairy**

to find out what's written in
silver on the shiny ribbon.